For Geraldine, Joe, Naomi,
Eddie, Laura and Isaac
M.R.

For Amelia
H.O.

First published 1989 by
Walker Books Ltd, 87 Vauxhall Walk
London SE11 5HJ

Exclusive edition for Premier Direct Group PLC.

Text © 1989 Michael Rosen
Illustrations © 1989 Helen Oxenbury

This book has been typeset in Veronan Light Educational

Printed in Italy

British Library Cataloguing in Publication Data
A catalogue record for this book
is available from the British Library.

ISBN 0-7445-8912-6

We're Going on a Bear Hunt

Retold by

Michael Rosen

Illustrated by

Helen Oxenbury

WALKER BOOKS

AND SUBSIDIARIES

LONDON · BOSTON · SYDNEY

We're going on a bear hunt.

We're going to catch a big one.

What a beautiful day!

We're not scared.

Uh-uh! Grass!

Long wavy grass.

We can't go over it.

We can't go under it.

Oh no!

We've got to go through it!

Swishy swashy!
Swishy swashy!
Swishy swashy!

We're going on a bear hunt.

We're going to catch a big one.

What a beautiful day!

We're not scared.

Uh-uh! A river!
A deep cold river.
We can't go over it.
We can't go under it.

Oh no!
We've got to go through it!

Splash splosh!
Splash splosh!
Splash splosh!

We're going on a bear hunt.

We're going to catch a big one.

What a beautiful day!

We're not scared.

Uh-uh! Mud!

Thick oozy mud.

We can't go over it.

We can't go under it.

Oh no!

We've got to go through it!

Squelch squerch!
Squelch squerch!
Squelch squerch!

We're going on a bear hunt.

We're going to catch a big one.

What a beautiful day!

We're not scared.

Uh-uh! A forest!

A big dark forest.

We can't go over it.

We can't go under it.

Oh no!

We've got to go through it!

Stumble trip!
Stumble trip!
Stumble trip!

We're going on a bear hunt.

We're going to catch a big one.

What a beautiful day!

We're not scared.

Uh-uh! A snowstorm!

A swirling whirling snowstorm.

We can't go over it.

We can't go under it.

Oh no!

We've got to go through it!

Hoooo woooo!
Hoooo woooo!
Hoooo woooo!

We're going on a bear hunt.

We're going to catch a big one.

What a beautiful day!

We're not scared.

Uh-uh! A cave!

A narrow gloomy cave.

We can't go over it.

We can't go under it.

Oh no!

We've got to go through it!

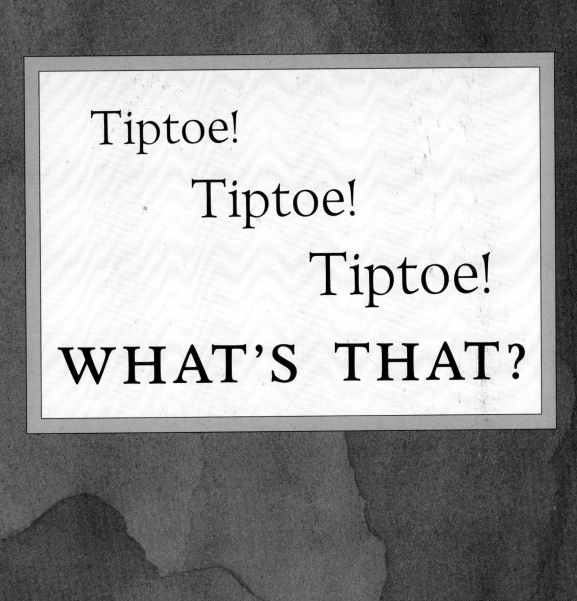

Tiptoe!

Tiptoe!

Tiptoe!

WHAT'S THAT?

One shiny wet nose!

Two big furry ears!

Two big goggly eyes!

IT'S A BEAR!!!!

Quick! Back through the cave! Tiptoe! Tiptoe! Tiptoe!

Back through the snowstorm! Hoooo wooooo! Hoooo wooooo!

Back through the forest! Stumble trip! Stumble trip! Stumble trip!

Back through the mud! Squelch squerch! Squelch squerch!

Back through the river! Splash splosh! Splash splosh! Splash splosh!

Back through the grass! Swishy swashy! Swishy swashy!

Get to our front door.

Open the door.

Up the stairs.

Oh no!

We forgot to shut the door.

Back downstairs.

Shut the door.

Back upstairs.

Into the bedroom.

Into bed.

Under the covers.

We're not going on

a bear hunt again.